Guji Guji

Text and illustrations copyright © 2003 by Chih-Yuan Chen

Originally published in 2003 by Hsin Yi Publications, Taipei, Taiwan, R.O.C.

All rights reserved.

English translation © Kane Miller

This edition first published in 2006 by

Gecko Press, P.O. Box 9335, Marion Square, Wellington 6141, New Zealand

www.geckopress.com

info@geckopress.com

National Library of New Zealand Cataloguing-in-Publication Data
Chen, Zhiyuan, 1975-
Guji Guji / by Chih-Yuan Chen ; illustrated by Chih-Yuan Chen.
First published in Taiwan, 2003.
ISBN 978-0-9582787-0-6
[1. Ducks—Fiction. 2. Crocodiles—Fiction. 3. Identity—Fiction.
4. Loyalty—Fiction.] I. Title.
813.6—dc 22

Text design by Archetype
Printed in China by Everbest

For more curiously good books, visit www.geckopress.com

Guji - Guji

by Chih-Yuan Chen

GECKO PRESS

An egg was rolling along the ground.
It rolled through the trees.
It rolled across the meadow.
It rolled all the way down the hill.

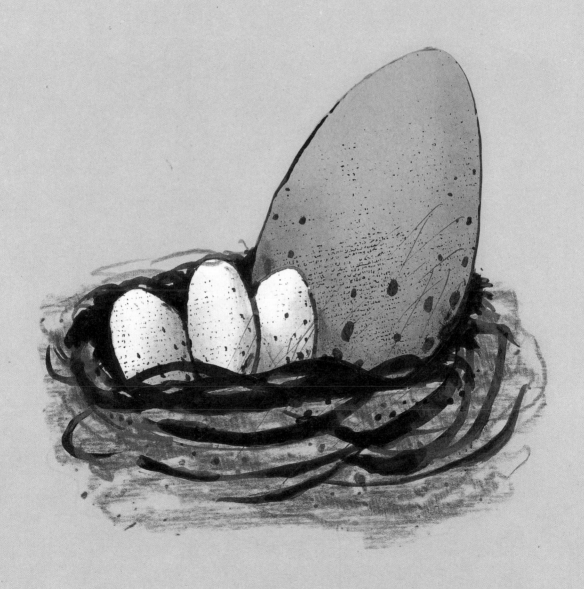

Finally, it rolled right into a duck's nest.

Mother Duck didn't notice. She was reading.

Soon enough, the eggs began to crack.
The first duckling to hatch had blue spots.
Mother Duck called him Crayon.
The second duckling had brown stripes.
"Zebra", Mother Duck decided.
The third duck was yellow, and Mother Duck
named him Moonlight.

A rather odd duckling hatched from the
fourth egg. "Guji Guji", he said, and
that became his name.

Mother Duck taught her four ducklings how to swim,
how to dive and how to waddle.

Guji Guji always learned more quickly than the others.
He was bigger and stronger, too.

But no matter how quick they were,
or what they looked like, Mother Duck
loved all her ducklings the same.

Then one terrible day, three crocodiles came
out of the lake. They looked a lot like Guji Guji.

The crocodiles were smiling, and when they
laughed with their mouths wide open,
the whole world could see their big, pointed teeth.

The three crocodiles saw Guji Guji and smiled some more.
"Look at that ridiculous crocodile.
He's walking like a duck!"

Guji Guji heard them. "I am not walking like a duck.
I *am* a duck!" he explained.

The crocodiles laughed. "Look at yourself!
No feathers, no beak, no big webbed feet!
What you have is blue-grey skin, sharp claws, pointed teeth
and the smell of bad crocodile.
You're just like us."

The first crocodile said, "Your blue-grey body lets you hide underwater without being seen, so you can get close to fat, delicious ducks."

The second crocodile said, "Big, sharp claws help you hold fat, delicious ducks tightly so they don't get away."

The third crocodile said, "Pointed teeth are necessary so you can chew fat, delicious ducks. Mmmm. Yum."

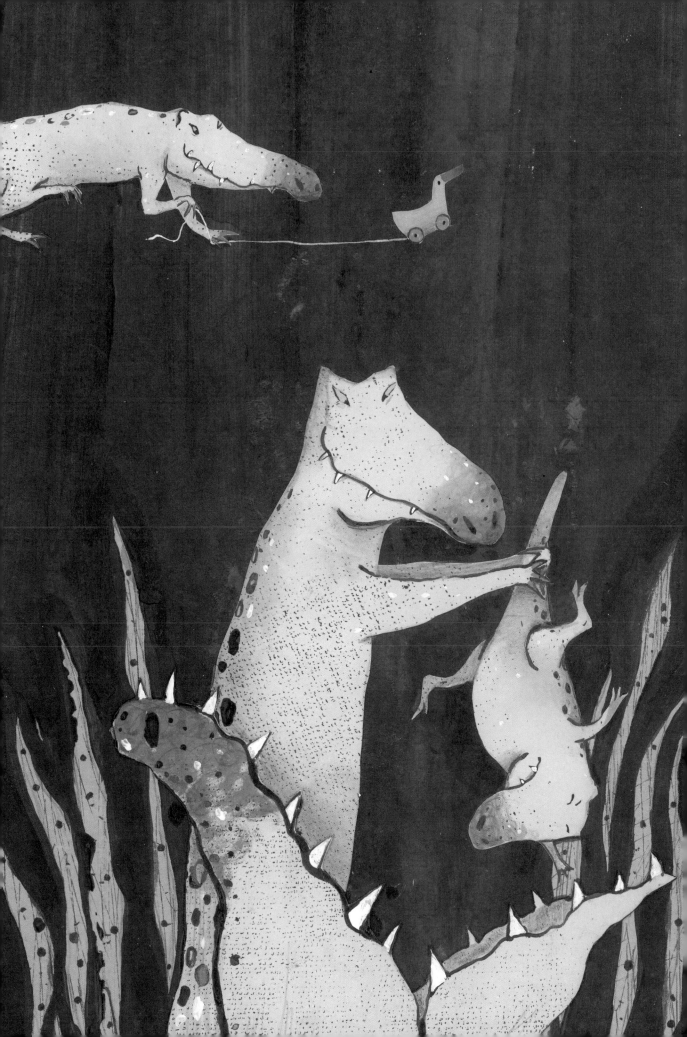

The three crocodiles grinned. "We know you live with the ducks.
Take them to the bridge tomorrow and practice diving.
We'll wait underneath with our mouths wide open."

"Why would I do that?" Guji Guji asked. "Why should I listen to you?"

"Because we are all crocodiles, and crocodiles help each other."
The bad crocodiles grinned again and vanished into the grass.

Guji Guji felt terrible.
He sat by the lake to think.
"Is it true? Am I a bad crocodile too?"
He looked down into the lake
and made a fierce face.
Guji Guji laughed.
He looked ridiculous.
"I am not a bad crocodile.
Of course, I'm not exactly
a duck either."

"But the three crocodiles are nasty, and they
want to eat my family. I must think of
a way to stop them."

Guji Guji thought and thought until
finally he thought up a good idea.
He went home happy and content.

That night, the three bad crocodiles sharpened
their pointed teeth, all the while thinking
of fat, delicious ducks.
They were ready for their feast.

The next day, Guji Guji did as he'd been told –
he took the flock of ducks to the bridge to practice diving.

The three bad crocodiles were waiting
for the ducks underneath the bridge.

But it wasn't fat, delicious ducks
that dropped from the bridge:
it was three big hard rocks!

The crocodiles bit down. "Crack! Crack! Crack!" went their pointed teeth.
The three bad crocodiles ran as fast as they could.
In barely a minute, they were nowhere to be seen!

Guji Guji had saved the ducks!
Guji Guji was the duck hero of the day!
That night, all the ducks danced and celebrated.

Guji Guji continued to live with Mother Duck,
Crayon, Zebra and Moonlight, and every day
he became a stronger and happier 'crocoduck'.